Chickpea Runs Away

Based on several true stories

By Sarat Colling

Illustrated by Vicky Bowes

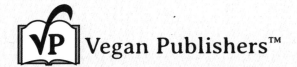 Vegan Publishers™

Chickpea Runs Away

Published by:
Vegan Publishers, Danvers, MA
www.veganpublishers.com

Typesetting: Nicola May Design

Artwork: Vicky Bowes

Printed in Malaysia

ISBN 978-1-940184-48-7

Dedicated to kids who love animals

On a big farm, in a vast land, there lived a little cow named Chickpea. She spent all of her time locked in a stall inside one of the huge barns there.

This farm wasn't a pleasant place to live. In fact, it wasn't a nice place at all: it was more like a factory than a farm. Chickpea and the other cows had never been allowed outside to see the blue sky, smell the fresh air, or chew on fresh green grass from the earth.

All day long, they didn't do much besides eat, chew their cud, and sleep.

I wish I could go outside, Chickpea thought. *I want to see the world and get out of my mucky stall.*

One day, Chickpea woke up to the sound of mooing and humans talking in loud voices. *What is going on?* Chickpea thought. She saw a group of cows being led outside. Outside! Why, no cow had been outside before! Chickpea was excited.

But then she saw that the cows were being led onto a big gray truck. There were many humans—men in heavy boots—tramping along, pushing and yelling at the cows to "Move it!" The cows disappeared into the truck and it drove away.

Chickpea's mommy lived in the stall next to hers. Chickpea didn't remember ever being able to touch her, but they spoke all the time: *Moo* this and *Moo* that. Chickpea's mommy told Chickpea that she loved her very much.

One day, while Chickpea was sleeping, she dreamed that her mommy came over and touched her nose to Chickpea's. It was wet and warm, and she felt full of love.

When Chickpea woke up, she discovered that her mommy was gone. She had left in the gray truck.

"She's not coming back," said a cow in a nearby stall. "They never do."

Chickpea lay down in her small stall and curled up tight. She wanted to go back to sleep and pretend like nothing had ever happened.

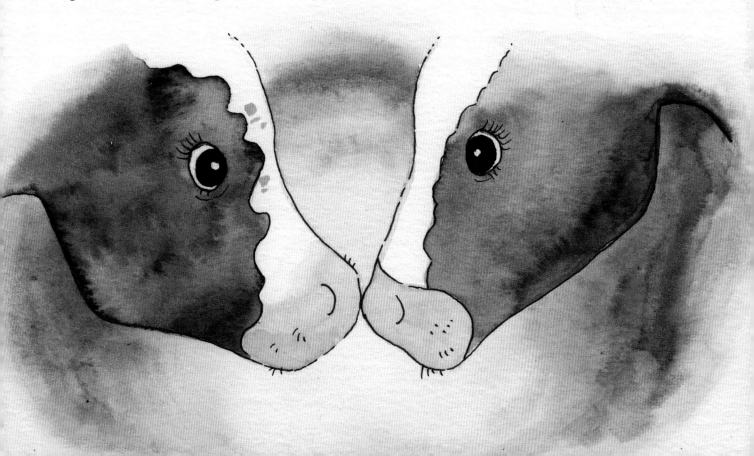

Winter came, and it was cold inside the barn where Chickpea lived. She missed Mommy very much, and sometimes Chickpea couldn't sleep at all. And so the long winter nights went on, day in and day out.

Finally, spring arrived. Little red robins fluttered into the barn, chirping and singing, bees buzzed here and there, and the sun, in what little light came into the barn, shone bright and warm.

One day, Chickpea heard the footfalls of the heavy boots the men wore:

boom, boom, boom!

A man Chickpea had never seen before came to Chickpea's stall and opened it. "You're coming with me," he said.

He led Chickpea out of the barn and into a pen in the yard. Chickpea felt her heart pound against her chest:

badump, badump, badump.

For the first time, Chickpea was outside. She took a deep breath. The air was fresh and crisp and clean. She looked to her right and saw lush green fields, moist with dew. She also saw trees and green rolling hills in the distance. Everything looked magical.

"They're going to take us away from here . . . to a terrible place," one cow said.

Another cow said: "They're going to take us in that truck."

Chickpea looked at the blue sky and the wide-open fields, which seemed to be calling her from the other side of the fence. There and then, she made up her mind. She wanted to find out more about the world. She didn't want to leave on the truck, and she didn't want to go somewhere terrible!

Chickpea started to run. She ran very fast and took a huge leap—right over the fence! Then she took off down the road.

"Where is she going?" said a farmer.

"Call the cops!" said another.

"Animal control!" said one of the men in boots.

Chickpea kept running, though, because she never ever wanted to go back in that pen inside that awful barn.

Chickpea ran so fast and so far, she eventually came to a wooded area. *What is this place?* she wondered. There were no fences or men with big trucks and heavy boots here.

As she moved into the forest, the earth became damp and soft beneath her hooves. The trees towered high above and shaded her from the hot sun. She soon came upon a stream and sipped some of the cool water.

Suddenly, she heard a voice.

"Hello there!" someone said.

Chickpea looked up and saw another animal. They didn't look like a cow . . . no, not like a cow at all. They were brown and slender.

"Who are you?" asked Chickpea.

"I'm Dahlia," said the animal. "Dahlia Deer. Pleased to meet you . . . Um, who are you?"

"I'm Chickpea. I came from the farm."

"The farm?" said Dahlia Deer. "Oh dear! How did you ever manage to escape that awful place? Come along with me and my herd. I'll show you where to find good grass to eat—ferns and shrubs, too."

"Thank you," said Chickpea.

Chickpea enjoyed living in the forest with the deer. But soon, spring gave way to summer, which turned to fall, and then the cold frosts of winter returned. Food became harder to find.

Whatever am I going to do? thought Chickpea.

One night, as big snowflakes fell from the sky, Chickpea wandered off into the woods. Suddenly, she smelled something yummy.

Sniffing, Chickpea followed her nose to a cabin at the edge of the forest. On a window ledge there lay five freshly baked pies. Chickpea had never seen a pie before, but they smelled delicious! So she gobbled one up, and it was tasty. After eating, she went back into the woods, where she fell asleep and dreamed about something wonderful.

In the dream, Chickpea's mommy came to her. She nestled up next to Chickpea, and they laid their heads down side by side. It felt safe and cozy.

When Chickpea awoke the next morning, there was a human staring down at her.

Who are you? thought Chickpea.

"You're not a deer!" said the human. She was a little girl in a blue coat with a red beanie hat on her head. "You're a cow!"

Chickpea swished her tail. "Moo!" she said. "*Moo!*"

Soon a little boy ran up. He wore an orange coat and a blue beanie hat. "You found a cow!" he said. "She must be the one who ate our vegan pie last night!"

Chickpea felt her heart begin to race. She began to wonder: *What if these humans want to hurt me like the others did?*

She ran away.

"Come back!" the children yelled.

But Chickpea did not come back.

The following day, Chickpea kept thinking about the two children. They seemed different.

Could there be nice humans in the world? Kind ones, gentle ones who would love her like her mommy once did?

Then, to her surprise, she realized she could smell those delicious pies again. *Can it be?* she wondered.

Chickpea followed the smell until she found a pie on the ground.

She chomped it up and then found another one not too far away. She found five pies before coming to the same cabin she'd found yesterday.

Then she saw the two little humans: the girl in the red beanie and the boy in the blue beanie. Little did she know it, but Chickpea had met the Chanterelle family, who spent their free time tending to the vegetable garden, baking vegan goodies, and volunteering at the local animal rescue center.

"I'm Maya," said the girl.

"And I'm Maya's brother," said the boy. "I'm Aster."

Chickpea thought she might run again. But there was something very kind in the children's eyes.

Suddenly, a voice called out, "Come inside, Aster and Maya!"

Chickpea started and turned around, ready to run away.

"Wait!" cried Maya. "Stop, little cow."

Chickpea turned back toward the children, her legs shaking from fear.

"Can we keep her, Mom?" said Maya. "She's by herself. She thinks she's a deer!"

The taller human was a mommy! Chickpea listened closely.

"Please, Mom," said Aster, "let us take care of her."

Mom was surprised to see a cow at their doorstep. "But, children," she said, "What do we know about keeping a cow?"

"We can learn," said Aster.

"And we can do our best," said Maya.

Mom called Dad, a nice man with a warm smile, who came outside. "What do you think?" she asked.

Dad looked at Chickpea and then at his children and then, finally, at Mom. "She sure looks like she has a story to tell!" he said. "I think we could give her a home."

"I think we can, too," said Mom. "Then it's agreed: the cow will stay with us . . . that is, if she wants to!"

The children ran and hugged their parents. Then they came and very gently wrapped their arms around Chickpea's neck.

This time, Chickpea did not run away.

These humans are kind and gentle, she thought. *I like it here; I'm going to stay.*

Chickpea lived the rest of her days at the vegetable farm with her new friends, who loved her very much. They made sure she always had fresh food and a comfortable place to sleep.

Sometimes, Dahlia and the other deer would pay Chickpea a visit. Other times, Chickpea would go walking alone in the woods to visit her deer friends—or find yummy blackberries to eat.

Chickpea never forgot her mommy or the other cows. But she found her heart filled with love and knew that running away from that frightful farm was the best decision she'd ever made.

The End